Hidenori Kusaka

I've completed my Galar Pokédex! It took a long time to capture 400 types of Pokémon, but it was worth it! I know you'll have a great time playing too!

Satoshi Yamamoto

What I like best about *Pokémon: Sword/Shield*:
① How the music changes during the battle when Pokémon go Dynamax! When the chorus kicks in, it's really exciting!

POKÉMON™
SWORD & SHIELD
1
STORY
Hidenori Kusaka
ART
Satoshi Yamamoto

Henry SWORD

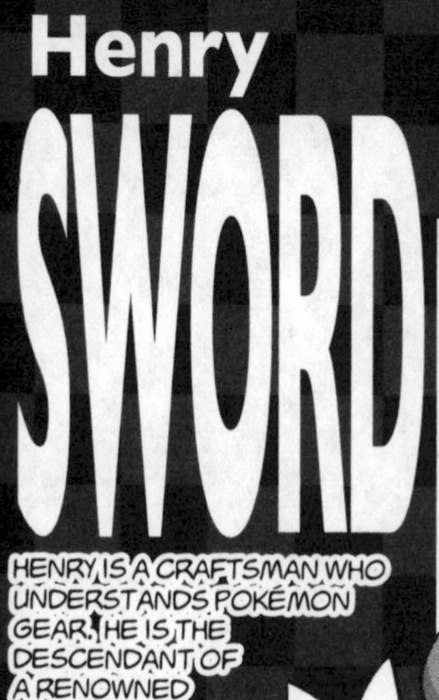

HENRY IS A CRAFTSMAN WHO UNDERSTANDS POKÉMON GEAR. HE IS THE DESCENDANT OF A RENOWNED SWORDSMITH AND USES FAMILY SECRETS TO ENHANCE THE GEAR HE COMES ACROSS.

Casey SHIELD

CASEY IS AN ACE COMPUTER HACKER WHO CAN CRACK ANY CODE AND GUESS ANY PASSWORD. SHE'S PROFESSOR MAGNOLIA'S ASSISTANT AND CHIPS IN AS THE TEAM'S DATA ANALYST.

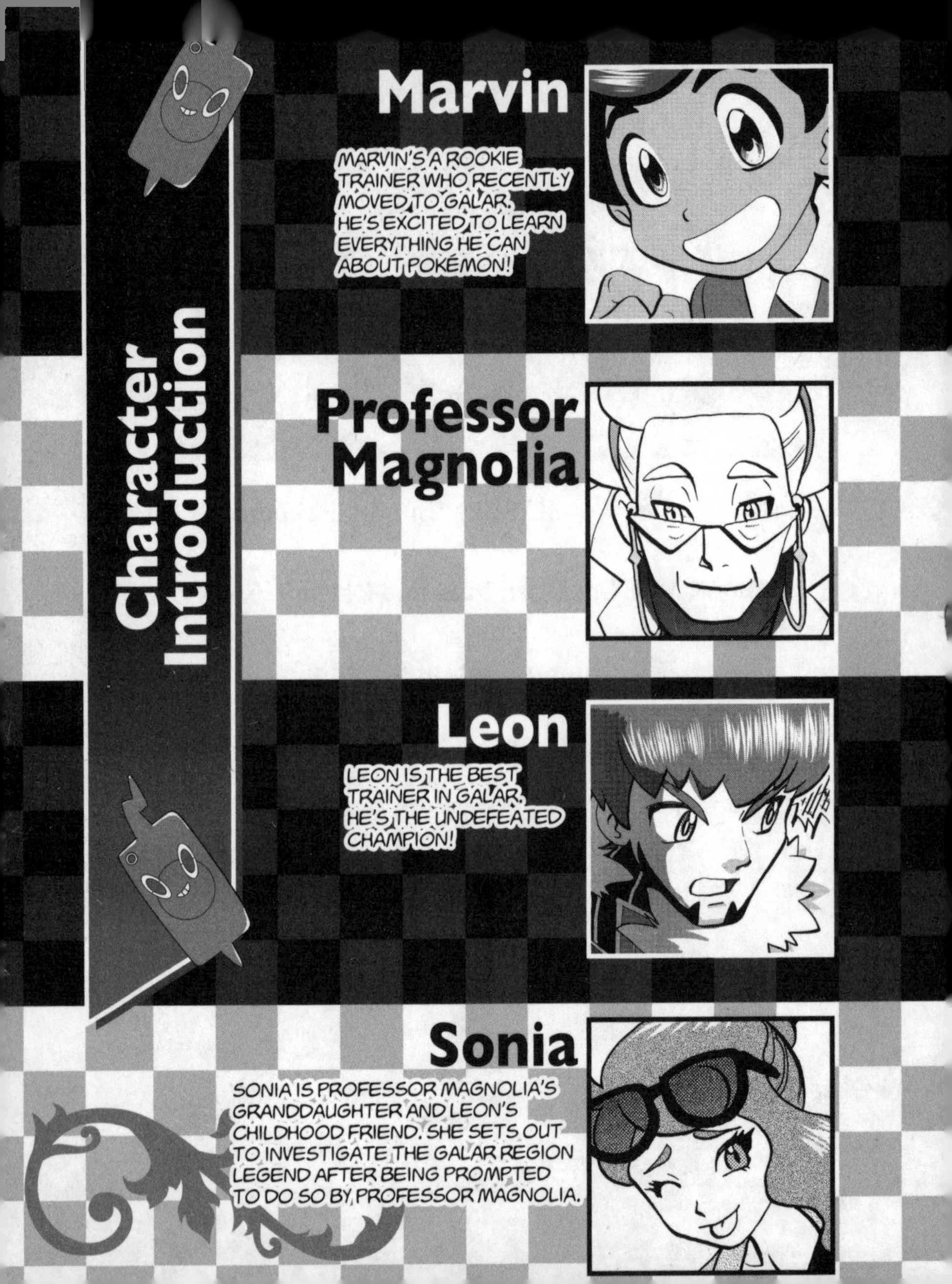
Character Introduction
Marvin
MARVIN'S A ROOKIE TRAINER WHO RECENTLY MOVED TO GALAR. HE'S EXCITED TO LEARN EVERYTHING HE CAN ABOUT POKÉMON!
Professor Magnolia
Leon
LEON IS THE BEST TRAINER IN GALAR. HE'S THE UNDEFEATED CHAMPION!
Sonia
SONIA IS PROFESSOR MAGNOLIA'S GRANDDAUGHTER AND LEON'S CHILDHOOD FRIEND. SHE SETS OUT TO INVESTIGATE THE GALAR REGION LEGEND AFTER BEING PROMPTED TO DO SO BY PROFESSOR MAGNOLIA.

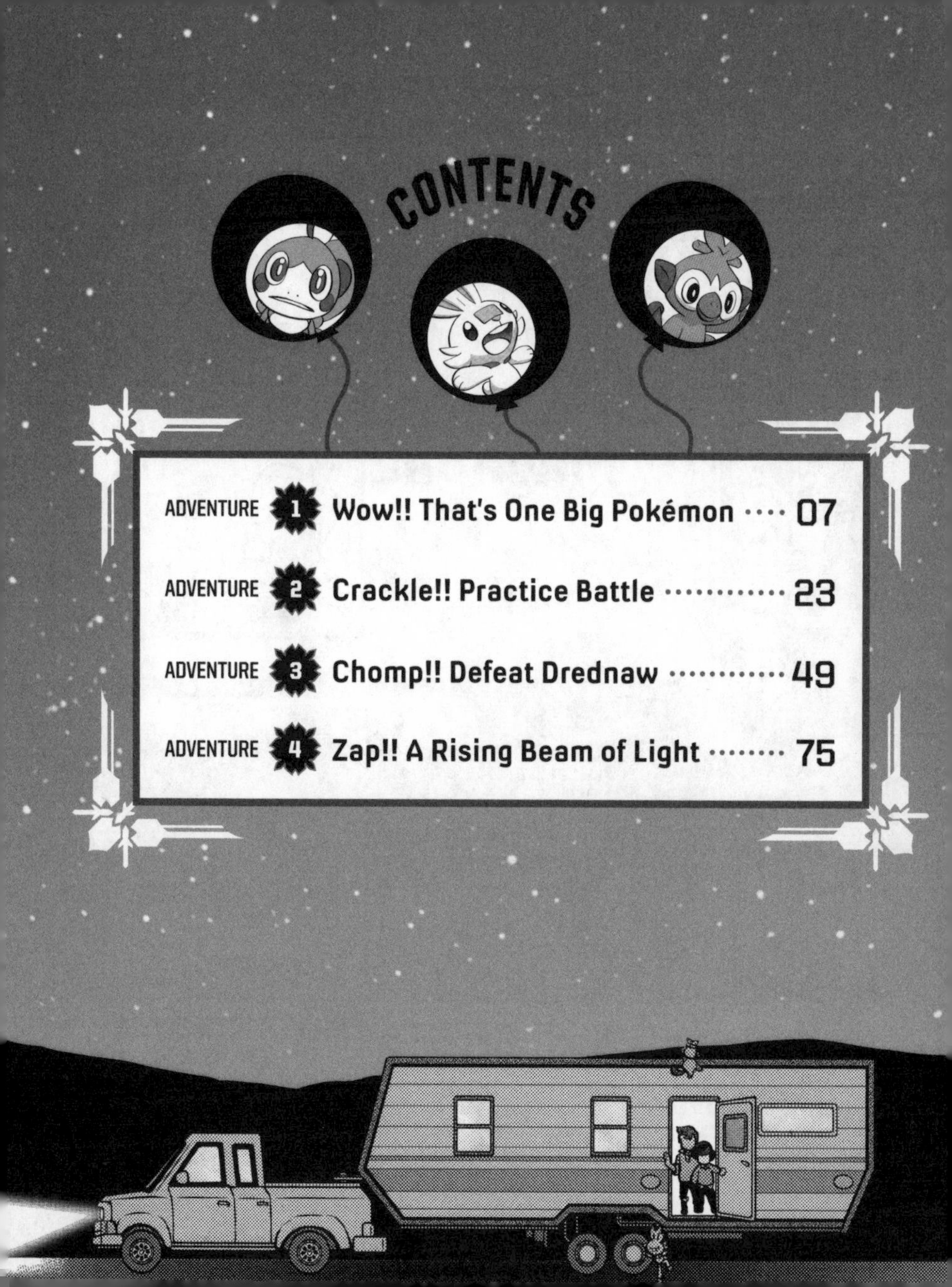

CONTENTS

ADVENTURE 1 Wow!! That's One Big Pokémon ···· 07

ADVENTURE 2 Crackle!! Practice Battle ············ 23

ADVENTURE 3 Chomp!! Defeat Drednaw ··········· 49

ADVENTURE 4 Zap!! A Rising Beam of Light ······· 75

WHAT? A ZIG-ZAGOON ?!
IT'S A ZIG-ZAGOON ?!
I HEARD THE GALAR REGION'S POKÉMON WERE A LITTLE DIFFERENT FROM THOSE IN OTHER REGIONS...
...BUT THEY'RE REALLY DIFFER-ENT!
ZIG ZIG ZIG
!
ZIG ZIG

Adventure 1 Wow!! That's One Big Pokémon..

IT DISAP-PEARED?
SHWOO...
WOW! ARE ALL GALAR PANGORO SO HUGE?!
AAAHH !!
THUNK
OOF.
HEY!

YOU OKAY?
I'LL GET YOU DOWN IN A JIFFY.
CARE TO LEND A WING?
FWOOSH
FWUMP

TAP
YOU SAVED MY LIFE!
AND YOU ARE...?
IT'S A POKÉMON CALLED SIRFETCH'D!
SO, HOW ARE YOU FEELING?
I'M OKAY.
BUT...
UH...
UMM...

DASH
WHAAAAAAT?!
EEK!
SHA

BOO!
SUR-PRISED?
WELL?!
WERE YOU SURPRISED OR NOT?!
STOMP STOMP
HEY!
CASEY SHIELD! THIS BOY HAS JUST HAD A HUGE SCARE.
DON'T TEASE HIM!

IS IT SCARY? I THINK BALL GUY LOOKS CUTE.
THAT'S NOT THE POINT...
SO, WHAT'S YOUR NAME?
I'M MARVIN.
MARVIN, EH?
WE WERE JUST ABOUT TO MAKE CAMP...
...WHEN YOU FELL OFF THAT CLIFF, SCREAMING.
SO WHAT HAPPENED?
WERE YOU TESTING YOUR COURAGE? OR DID A BULLY DARE YOU TO JUMP? I KNOW, A SCARY POKÉMON WAS CHASING YOU AROUND AND...!
CASEY, HUSH!
NO!
THERE WAS A HUGE PANGORO! THEN IT DISAP-PEARED...
...SO I WENT OVER TO THE CLIFF TO GET A CLOSER LOOK...
...

DON'T CALL ME MARV...
AND WHAT DO YOU MEAN?
MY BAD, MARV!
THIS IS ALL YOUR FAULT, CASEY.
OOPSY!
SHIELD, SLOW DOWN!
WHAT I MEAN IS I WAS TESTING OUT MY DYNAMAX SIMULATOR BECAUSE PEOPLE HARDLY COME HERE, SO I THOUGHT IT'D BE FINE! I MADE THE DYNAMAX SIMULATOR MYSELF—IT'S A HOLOGRAM, A STEREOSCOPIC IMAGE! PRETTY AMAZING, HUH?! I MADE IT LOOK LIKE A HUGE POKÉMON, BUT ACTUALLY...
SCREECH
BUT YOU HAVE TO BE QUIET! DON'T RAISE YOUR VOICE, OKAY?!
THIS WAY!
OH SURE!
I THINK IT'S TIME TO THANK THE PERSON AND THE POKÉMON WHO SAVED ME...

HENRY, IT'S ME!
MARVIN WANTED TO THANK YOU AND SIRFETCH'D!!
THIS IS QUIET?!
WHAT?

HEY, HENRY!
IS THIS THE SAME GUY?
SORRY, CASEY! WHEN DID YOU COME IN?
HEY, MARVIN! ARE YOU ALL RIGHT?
YES. THANK YOU VERY MUCH FOR SAVING ME.
HENRY, YOU'RE CONCEN-TRATING TOO HARD!
SO WHAT WERE YOU DOING?
I WAS FIXING SIR-FETCH'D'S LEEK SPEAR.

HENRY IS A GEAR CRAFTSMAN.
GEAR?
FARFETCH'D'S SPEAR, MAROWAK'S BONE, SAMUROTT'S SEAMITAR, DELPHOX'S WAND, GURDURR'S STEEL BEAM...
THAT'S ALL GEAR—OR AT LEAST THAT'S WHAT SWORD CALLS IT.
I HAVE TO CALL IT SOMETHING...
GEAR IS WHAT YOU CALL THE TOOLS POKÉMON USE IN THEIR DAILY LIVES AND BATTLES.
BUT THEY SUFFER FROM WEAR AND TEAR, LIKE ANYTHING ELSE.
MY JOB IS TO KEEP THEM IN PERFECT CONDITION.
GROOKEY, COME HERE.
THIS IS THE CHIMP POKÉMON, GROOKEY.
THE STICK IT'S HOLDING IS A PIECE OF GEAR TOO.
IF I DO THIS...
SHFF
THE STICK BECOMES HARDER AND STRONGER.
HUH!

THAT MAKES SENSE! SOUND GOOD, MARVIN?
USE THE VR DECK. IF YOU SURPRISE SOMEONE ELSE, YOU MIGHT CAUSE ANOTHER ACCIDENT.
HOLD IT, CASEY.
NOW COME SEE MY DYNAMAX SIMULATOR!
MAYBE TELL ME WHAT THE DYNAMAX SIMULATOR IS FIRST?
ONCE YOU'RE JACKED INTO THE SIMULATOR, YOU'LL UNDER-STAND EVERY-THING!
FIRST THINGS FIRST– THE VR DECK!
SWIP
WHOA!
TRY AND KEEP UP, MARV!
I JUST MOVED HERE, SO I DON'T KNOW ANYTHING ABOUT THIS REGION.

OH WOW!
GREAT, NOW LET'S FIGHT! I'LL USE MY SCORBUNNY! YOU DON'T HAVE A POKÉMON, DO YOU, MARVIN?
YOU CAN FIGHT WITH MY SIRFETCH'D.
UM... WAIT A MINUTE!

I DON'T EVEN KNOW YOUR FULL NAMES!
I BARELY KNOW EITHER OF YOU!
I'M CASEY SHIELD.
I GUESS YOU COULD CALL ME JUST SHIELD, BUT IT'S PER-FECTLY FINE TO CALL ME JUST CASEY!
OH! I'M HENRY SWORD.
CALL ME HENRY OR SWORD OR WHATEVER YOU LIKE.
I'M PROFESSOR MAGNOLIA.
I DON'T THINK WE NEED TO BE ON A FIRST-NAME BASIS, YOUNG MAN.
OF COURSE, PROFES-SOR!
THAT'S TOO MANY NAMES ANYWAY!

THE SECRETS OF DYNAMAX, PART 1

Professor Magnolia

The Pokémon of Galar can become enormous by Dynamaxing. Professor Magnolia discovered the amazing scientific process behind this regional phenomenon ten years ago.

▲Professor Magnolia's research is still ongoing.

Adventure 2 Crackle!! Practice Battle

ALL RIGHT.
SO...
HENRY SWORD...
...AND CASEY SHIELD ...
...AND PROFES-SOR MAGNOLIA.
NOW PUT ON THE VR DECK ALREADY!
LET'S GET YOU JACKED INTO THE SIMULA-TOR.
AUGH!

CASEY, WE NEED TO WEAR THEM TOO.
WELL, DUH!
YOU TOO, EVERY-ONE!
SWOOP...
READY, MARVIN?
READY FOR WHAT?
TO DEFEAT THIS PANGORO IN A POKÉMON BATTLE, OF COURSE!
BUT I'VE NEVER HAD A POKÉMON BATTLE BEFORE!
SERI-OUSLY?!
I KNOW THE THEORY!
EVERY POKÉMON HAS SPECIAL MOVES THAT WEAKEN THEIR OPPONENT.
IF A TRAINER WANTS TO CAPTURE THAT POKÉMON, THEY MUST THROW A POKÉ BALL BEFORE THE POKÉMON IS UNABLE TO BATTLE.

OKAY.
BOOT IT UP, PROFES- SOR!
LET'S TRY TOGETHER.
THAT'S RIGHT!
AIEEE!
THUNGKT!
GWOOSH
WHAT ?!
THOSE WERE HIGH FREQUENCY ELECTRIC WAVES! I THOUGHT IT WOULD BE A MORE REALISTIC EXPERIENCE IF YOU FELT THE ATTACK. DON'T WORRY, YOU WON'T DIE IF YOU'RE HIT! TRUE, IT DOES HURT, SO THE SHOCK MIGHT...
THAT STUNG!
HEY, WHERE ARE YOU GOING?

PROFESSOR, COULD YOU PAUSE THE BATTLE?
HALT...
MARVIN, WHY DO YOU KNOW THE RULES OF A POKÉMON BATTLE?
AND WHY DIDN'T YOU RUN AWAY WHEN YOU SAW THAT HUGE PANGORO?
ONE DAY, I WANT TO CATCH MY OWN POKÉMON, AND GO ON A JOURNEY...
...AND TRAIN IN THE POKÉMON GYMS TOO!
THEN YOU NEED TO PRACTICE!
GYM BATTLES IN GALAR ARE DYNAMAX BATTLES!
RESTART, PROFESSOR!
BWOOSH!!

GROOKEY, USE LEAFAGE!
SCORBUNNY, USE EMBER!
CHOOM
CHOOM
KRRSHAA
SHUK SHUK SHUK SHUK
LOOK CLOSELY.
THERE IS ALWAYS A PAUSE BETWEEN THE ATTACK AND DEFENSE.
THAT'S TO PREPARE THE POKÉMON'S NEXT MOVES.
I LEARNED ABOUT IT AT THE TRAINERS' SCHOOL.
THEN YOU MAKE YOUR NEXT ATTACK.
AND YOU KEEP DOING THAT UNTIL YOU WIN!
AND THEN THERE'S TYPE ADVANTAGES TO CONSIDER.

SIRFETCH'D IS A FIGHTING TYPE. IT CAN USE A MOVE CALLED METEOR ASSAULT.
PANGORO IS A DARK TYPE.
THEN I'M AT AN ADVANTAGE WITH THE TYPE!
THAT WON'T BE ENOUGH!
WHEN POKÉMON DYNAMAX, THEY'RE TOUGHER, AND THEIR MOVES ARE STRONGER.
IF YOU KEEP YOUR DISTANCE, YOU'LL BECOME AN EASY TARGET.
YOU NEED TO HAVE THE COURAGE TO RUSH UP TO IT.
GULP...
GO ON.
PAP
AHHHHHH!

THUNK
OW!!
IT REALLY HURTS!
I DON'T WANT TO DO THIS!
POKÉMON BATTLES ARE SCARY!
SIR-FETCH'D ...
...!
THE PAUSE!
GWOO

SIR-
FETCH'D!
IT'S
TIME!
METEOR
ASSAULT!!
SLLSSH!!

YOU DID IT, MARV!
YOUR TIMING WAS PERFECT.
SIRFETCH'D PROTECTED ME...
A PARTNERSHIP WITH A POKÉMON...
I LEARNED ABOUT IT AT SCHOOL, BUT THIS IS THE REAL THING...
I WAS AN HONORS STUDENT AT THE TRAINERS' SCHOOL IN MY PREVIOUS REGION.
BUT I COULDN'T FIT INTO THE SCHOOL IN GALAR...
THAT'S WHY I HAVEN'T BEEN GOING TO SCHOOL. AND I DIDN'T HAVE THE COURAGE TO SET OUT ON MY OWN JOURNEY...
BUT NOW...
...I CAN'T WAIT TO SET OUT!

WE CAN DO THAT ON THE WAY!
I SHOULD PROBABLY TELL MY PARENTS...
THEN COME WITH US!
WHAT?
YOU DON'T MIND, DO YOU, PROFES-SOR?
DON'T DISAP-POINT SWORD!
COME ON, COME ON!!
LET'S GO!!
I'M SURE I CAN GET YOUR PARENTS' PERMIS-SION.
I'M A WELL-KNOWN RESEARCHER HERE IN GALAR.
VRROOM

YOU WON'T REGRET IT!
I CAN'T BELIEVE IT. SHE SAID I CAN GO...
UH-HUH... SURE, MOM... THANKS. TALK TO YOU LATER!
MY PARENTS WANTED TO KNOW HOW I MET THE AUTHORITY ON DYNAMAX RESEARCH!
IT'S ALL THANKS TO YOU.
PEOPLE THINK THE GALAR REGION'S POWER SPOTS ENABLE POKÉMON TO DYNAMAX AND BECOME GIGANTIC...
BUT IT'S NOT JUST THE LOCATION! MANY OTHER CONDITIONS ARE NEEDED FOR A POKÉMON TO GO DYNAMAX.
WHAT DO YOU MEAN ...?
BUT THAT'S NOT THE ONLY REASON I MADE IT!
I HAD CASEY CREATE THE SIMULATOR TO HELP ME WITH MY RESEARCH.

ISN'T IT OBVIOUS?! SO WE CAN TRAIN FOR OUR GYM CHALLENGES!
YOU'RE GOING TO CHALLENGE THE GYMS?!
WE WANT TO.
BUT IT'S DIFFICULT TO QUALIFY!
BAM BAM BAM
WHERE I'M FROM, ANYONE CAN CHALLENGE A GYM AS LONG AS THEY'RE A TRAINER...
IN GALAR, YOU NEED A SKILLED TRAINER'S RECOMMENDATION TO QUALIFY FOR GYM CHALLENGES.
YOU CAN ALSO GET RECOMMENDATIONS FROM THE CHAMPION AND MEMBERS OF THE POKÉMON LEAGUE COMMITTEE.
WHO'S THE CHAMPION OF GALAR?

I THINK THERE'S A TV SPECIAL ON THE UP-COMING GYM CHALLENGES TONIGHT...
THE CHAMPION IS SCHEDULED TO APPEAR IN IT!
FIRST WE NEED TO MAKE SOME DINNER.
THERE'S TIME BEFORE THE SHOW STARTS IF WE HURRY!
THE CHALLENGE IS TO TRAVEL TO ALL EIGHT STADIUMS AND DEFEAT THEIR GYM LEADERS!
TRAINERS WHO PASS THE GYM CHALLENGE ...
...MAY PARTICIPATE IN THE ANNUAL TOURNAMENT TO DETERMINE THE LEAGUE CHAMPION!
THE CHAMPION CUP!

AND NOW, I'LL INTRODUCE YOU TO OUR GUEST!
SINCE MAKING HIS DEBUT, THE CURRENT CHAMPION HASN'T LOST A SINGLE BATTLE...
HA A A
MEET LEON!
ABOUT THAT...
THE CHAMPION HASN'T ARRIVED IN WEDGEHURST YET?
IT SEEMS A GROUP OF WOOLOO HAVE WANDERED ONTO THE TRAIN TRACKS OUTSIDE WEDGEHURST...
...AND NOW THERE ARE DELAYS ON THE LINE...
THE TRACKS HEADING FOR MOTOSTOKE JUST OUTSIDE WEDGEHURST...
THAT'S CLOSE TO HERE!
THERE IT IS!

KRRM!!
WHAT IS THAT?!
A VIKAVOLT VIDEO DRONE!
FOUND HIM!
IT'S LEON!
HE'S BEING CHASED! WE SHOULD HELP HIM!
LOOK CLOSER!
!
A CHARIZARD?!

ROLL ROLL ROLL
THAT'S HOW THEY'RE GETTING THE WOOLOO AWAY FROM THE TRAIN TRACKS!
LEON IS LEADING THE WOOLOO, AND THE CHARIZARD IS HERDING THEM.
RRRMMBLL
I WISH I KNEW WHAT'S DRAWING THE WOOLOO TO THE TRAIN TRACKS...
IT'S BEEN LIKE THIS FOR AGES, LEON.
ANOTHER GROUP HAS ESCAPED!
WHAT?!
NOT AGAIN!

AND YOU TWO ARE...?
THE PROBLEM ISN'T THE TRAIN TRACKS. IT'S WHAT'S INSIDE THE FENCE...
RIGHT?
...
I'M HENRY SWORD. AND WE'D LIKE TO HELP.
I'M CASEY SHIELD!
SWIP!
CASEY, I'LL BE COUNTING ON YOUR NAVIGATION.
GOT-CHA!
HENRY, ON YOUR LEFT! THERE'S A CLOUD OF SMOKE!
KEEP GOING!

IT'S AN OBSTA-GOON!
GO RIGHT!
THAT'S THE LAST OF THEM!
POM
SLAM!
SO THAT POKÉMON WAS SCARING THE WOOLOO INSIDE THE FENCE!
WHAK!!

HE USED OB-STRUCT!
THE LEEK SPEAR DIDN'T AFFECT IT!
IN THAT CASE...
CONFUSE IT WITH YOUR QUICK STEPS!
SHOOO
LOOK!
IT CAN'T TELL WHICH ATTACK TO BLOCK!
VSH

SLAM!
ROLL ROLL
ALL CLEAR!

YOU BETTER HURRY TO THE TV STATION! THERE'S STILL TIME!
NO PROB-LEM!
THANKS!
NICE TO SEE YOU AGAIN, LEON.
PROFES-SOR MAGNO-LIA!
ARE THESE YOUR FRIENDS?
YES, THEY'RE HELPING ME WITH MY RESEARCH.
HOW'S SONIA DOING?
SHE'S BEEN BUSY TRAVELING.
PLEASE TELL HER SHE SHOULD COME SEE THE CHAMPION-SHIP CUP. IT STARTS NEXT WEEK.
OKAY! BUT YOU SHOULD HURRY NOW.

TOOOOOT
PROFES-SOR, YOU KNOW THE CHAMPION?
NO BIGGIE.
THE PLAN WORKED!
YEP!
PERFECT TIMING, PROFES-SOR!
WHAT DO YOU MEAN?
LEON WOULDN'T HAVE HAD ANY TROUBLE DEFEATING OBSTAGOON AND HERDING THE WOOLOO BY HIMSELF.
BUT HE'LL REMEMBER HOW WE STEPPED UP TO HELP!
SQUEEE

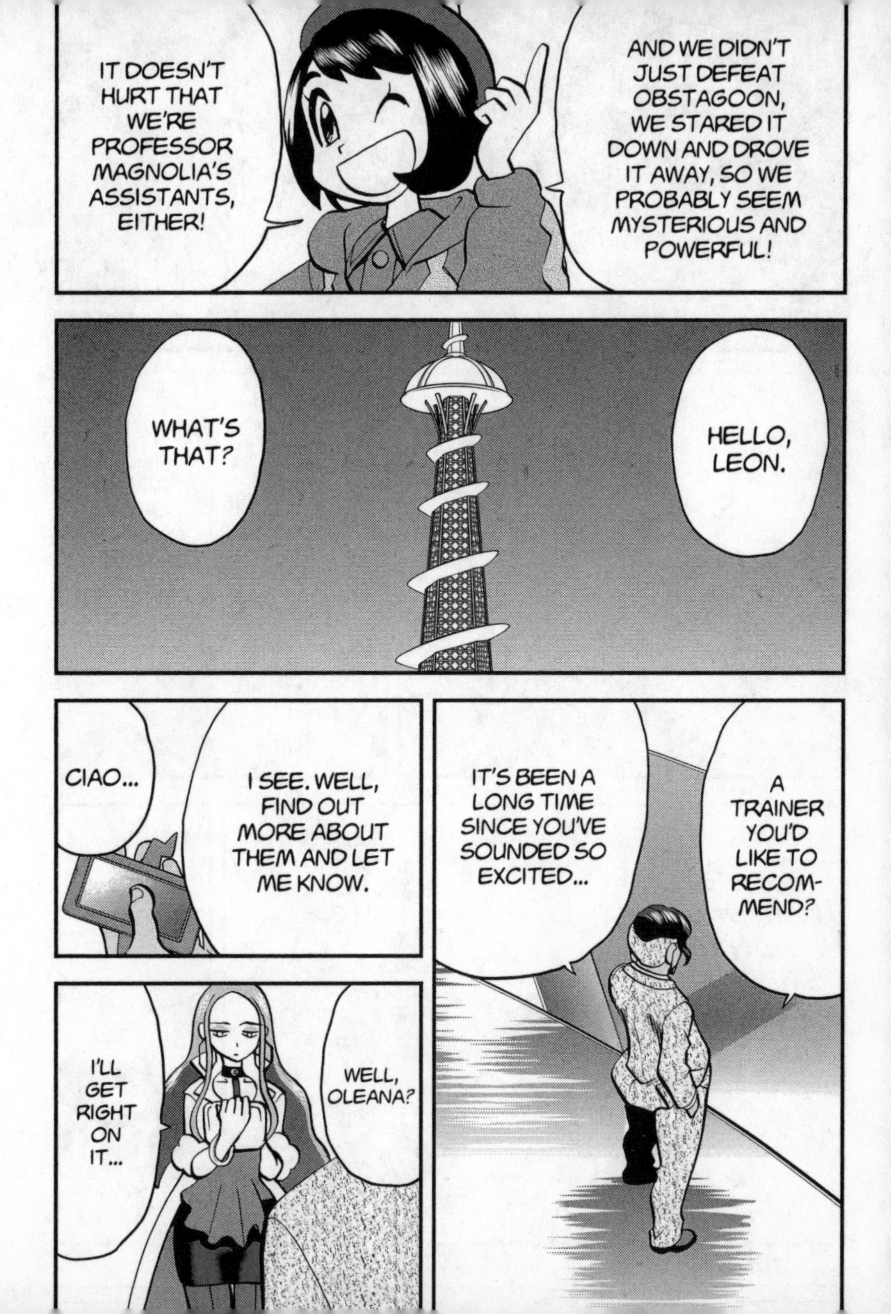
AND WE DIDN'T JUST DEFEAT OBSTAGOON, WE STARED IT DOWN AND DROVE IT AWAY, SO WE PROBABLY SEEM MYSTERIOUS AND POWERFUL!
IT DOESN'T HURT THAT WE'RE PROFESSOR MAGNOLIA'S ASSISTANTS, EITHER!
HELLO, LEON.
WHAT'S THAT?
A TRAINER YOU'D LIKE TO RECOM-MEND?
IT'S BEEN A LONG TIME SINCE YOU'VE SOUNDED SO EXCITED...
I SEE. WELL, FIND OUT MORE ABOUT THEM AND LET ME KNOW.
CIAO...
WELL, OLEANA?
I'LL GET RIGHT ON IT...

CHAIRMAN ROSE.
WHAT? LEON DIDN'T SHOW UP?!
THE TRAIN SHOULD HAVE GOTTEN HIM THERE IN PLENTY OF TIME!
LEON'S ALWAYS HAD AN AWFUL SENSE OF DIRECTION...
HOW DID I END UP BACK HERE?!
HMM?

▲The Power Spot Detector is used to find Power Spots!

Power Spots

A Pokémon needs to be in a Power Spot in order to Dynamax!

Adventure 3 Chomp!! Defeat Drednaw

⑪
⑫
⑬
⑭
⑪ Sink
Shelf contains a big pot for campfire curry cookouts.
⑫ Bathroom
No rest stops needed! There's a shower and a toilet.
⑬ Living room and bedroom
Fold up the table and open out the sofa to create Shield and the professor's bed!
⑭ TV
AWAKE AT LAST!
GOOD MORNING!

WHAT'S THIS PLACE?
MY LAB! THIS IS WHERE I WRITE PROGRAMS FOR THE DYNAMAX SIMULATOR AND ANALYZE THE DATA!
WHAT WAS THAT YOU JUST SAID ABOUT 14 SECONDS?
THAT'S THE TIME IT TOOK LEON TO RETURN THE WOOLOO!

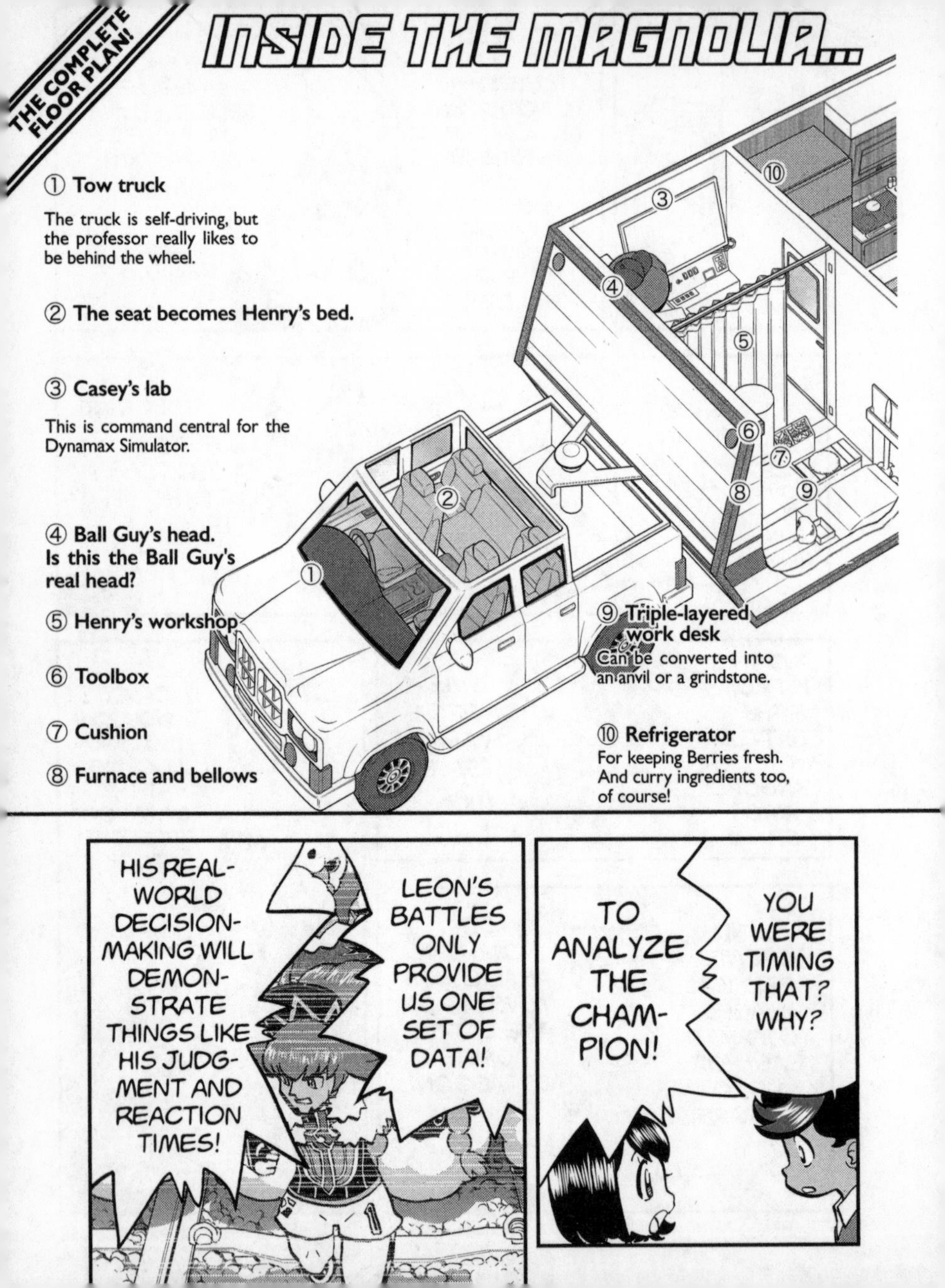

THE COMPLETE FLOOR PLAN!
INSIDE THE MAGNOLIA...
① Tow truck
The truck is self-driving, but the professor really likes to be behind the wheel.
② The seat becomes Henry's bed.
③ Casey's lab
This is command central for the Dynamax Simulator.
④ Ball Guy's head. Is this the Ball Guy's real head?
⑤ Henry's workshop
⑥ Toolbox
⑦ Cushion
⑧ Furnace and bellows
⑨ Triple-layered work desk
Can be converted into an anvil or a grindstone.
⑩ Refrigerator
For keeping Berries fresh. And curry ingredients too, of course!
YOU WERE TIMING THAT? WHY?
TO ANALYZE THE CHAMPION!
LEON'S BATTLES ONLY PROVIDE US ONE SET OF DATA!
HIS REAL-WORLD DECISION-MAKING WILL DEMONSTRATE THINGS LIKE HIS JUDGMENT AND REACTION TIMES!

SO WE SHOULD HAVE JUST RECORDED HIM DRIVING THE OBSTAGOON AWAY. BUT...
IT'S ALSO IMPORTANT TO GET HIM TO NOTICE US! WE WON'T GET ANYWHERE UNLESS WE GET PERMISSION TO TAKE PART IN THE GYM BATTLES!
WHERE IS PROFESSOR MAGNOLIA?
DRIVING!
BUT SHE OUGHT TO LET THE TRUCK DRIVE ITSELF!
SHE'S ALWAYS LOVED TO DRIVE CARS...
...AND RACE ALONG MOUNTAIN TRAILS.
CASEY, WOULD YOU MIND LOOKING AT THE DATA FOR SIRFETCH'D, TOO?
YOU BET!
THIS IS FROM WHEN IT SAVED MARVIN!
AND THIS IS FROM THE BATTLE WITH THE PANGORO PROGRAM!
SO NOW I CAN ANALYZE ITS MOVES FROM THE BATTLE AGAINST OSTAGOON...
...AND CREATE GRAPHICAL IMAGES TO MAKE IT EASY FOR US TO COMPARE...

LOOK— THE TIME SIRFETCH'D TOOK TO HURL THE SPEAR AT A TARGET HAS SHORTENED!
THAT MAINTE-NANCE YOU DID MUST HAVE WORKED!
I JUST MADE THE ANGLE ON THE TIP OF THE SPEAR A LITTLE SHARPER.
AND THE DRAG DECREASED! YOUR IDEA TO SOAK IT IN SPRING WATER SEEMS TO HAVE HELPED TOO. THE DENSITY OF THE LEEK HAS INCREASED SUBSTANTIALLY! MAYBE BECAUSE OF THE MINERALS IN THE WATER...
NEXT UP, DURA-BILITY!
HM. JUDGING FROM HOW IT DEFORMED AFTER USING SLAM...
RTTLE RTTLE
WUMP

PROFESSOR, WHAT HAPPENED?
WE HAVE A FLAT TIRE.
I'LL TAKE A LOOK.
I'LL HELP TOO!
HOLD IT! YOU DON'T KNOW WHAT'S OUT THERE!
HUH?
A WILD POKÉMON COULD HAVE CAUSED THE FLAT!
SHUFF

KLAK
KLAK
COAST'S CLEAR!
THOK!
IT'S THIS TIRE. I'LL TAKE A LOOK AT THE PUNCTURE. COULD YOU GIVE US A LIGHT, SCOR-BUNNY?
THE PUNCTURE WAS MADE BY RUNNING OVER SOMETHING HARD AND SHARP!
HEY, SOBBLE, WHAT ARE YOU DOING OUTSIDE ?!

PLIP PLIP...
WAARG
IT WANTS TO HELP!
BUT SOBBLE DOESN'T HAVE A TRAINER YET!
IF IT BUMPS INTO A STRONG WILD POKÉMON, IT WON'T KNOW HOW TO RUN AWAY OR FIGHT!
WHY ARE YOU CRYING?
YOU START-ED IT!
WHAT?

IT'S SOBBLE. ITS TEARS ARE SAID TO PACK THE CHEMICAL PUNCH OF A HUNDRED ONIONS.
SNIFF SNIFF... IS THAT SO.
SOBBLE, LET'S WAIT INSIDE THE TRUCK TOGETHER.
KRRSHH
KRRSH
WHAT ?!
DON'T YOU WANT TO COME WITH ME?
I FEEL LIKE CRYING AGAIN.
BOOOSH

DRED-NAW! THREE OF THEM!
THE SHAPE OF THE PUNC-TURE MATCH-ES ITS SHELL!
WE MUST HAVE RUN OVER ONE!
SHF
SHF

MARVIN, GET INSIDE!
BYE!
WHOA!
CHOMP
LOOKS LIKE THEY'RE GONNA ATTACK.
SHIELD, WHAT KIND OF POKÉMON IS IT?
UH...
I DUNNO.
I'M SURE IT'S A DREDNAW...
...
BUT THE TYPE SLIPPED MY MIND!

MAYBE IT'LL COME TO ME WHILE WE'RE FIGHTING!
SCOR-BUNNY!
SEPARATE THE THREE OF THEM!
TMP
TMP
THOK
TMP
TMP
TMP
TMP
TMP
TMP
WHOMP!
TMP
IT'S SO FAST...
...ITS FEET ARE ON FIRE!
TALK ABOUT HOT-FOOTING IT!

MARVIN, GET INSIDE!
BYE!
WHOA!
PRUCHOMP
LOOKS LIKE THEY'RE GONNA ATTACK.
SHIELD, WHAT KIND OF POKÉMON IS IT?
UH...
I DUNNO.
I'M SURE IT'S A DREDNAW...
...
BUT THE TYPE SLIPPED MY MIND!

TMP
TMP
THOK
TMP
TMP
TMP
SEPARATE THE THREE OF THEM!
SCOR-BUNNY!
MAYBE IT'LL COME TO ME WHILE WE'RE FIGHTING!
TMP
TMP
WHOMP!
TALK ABOUT HOT-FOOTING IT!
...ITS FEET ARE ON FIRE!
IT'S SO FAST...

BWOOSH
RIGHT! THE PADS ON THE BACK OF ITS FEET ARE PRE-HEATED AND READY TO FIGHT!
GO!
SIZZLE
SIZZLE
GOODNESS GRACIOUS, DREDNAW'S ON FIRE!
SCOR-BUNNY, GET 'EM!

CLOMP
CLOMP
CLOMP
CLOMP
BUT HOW COULD IT CATCH UP WITH SCOR-BUNNY?!
WOOSH
HENRY, CASEY IS IN TROU...
KCH
OH NO! HENRY'S IN TROUBLE TOO!
KRCH
KCH
CH

THEIR SMART-PHONES ARE INSIDE ON THE TABLE. GO GET THEM!
MARVIN!
HUUH!
WHAT IF I CAN'T THROW THEM FAR ENOUGH?
DON'T WORRY!
SWSH
I dunno...
I DID MY BEST...

SHUP!
WHAAAAAT?!
WHIZZ
PRO-FES-SOR?
HAVE YOU HEARD OF THE POKÉMON CALLED ROTOM?
ROTOM IS A POKÉMON THAT LOVES TO ENTER ELECTRIC APPLIANCES LIKE VACUUM CLEANERS AND REFRIGERATORS...
...AND IN GALAR, WE PUT THEM IN OUR SMART-PHONES.

AND TONIGHT, I INSTALLED A POKÉDEX ON THEIR ROTOM PHONES.
A POKÉ-DEX!
THEN HENRY AND CASEY ARE...
... POKÉDEX HOLDERS!

Bite Pokémon
Type
WATER
ROCK
Height
3'03"
Weight
254.6 lbs
Number Battled
3
With jaws that can shear through steel rods, this highly aggressive Pokémon chomps down on its unfortunate prey.
Bite Pokémon
Type
WATER
ROCK
Height
3'03"
Weight
254.6 lbs
Number Battled
1
This Pokémon rapidly extends its retractable neck to sink its sharp fangs into distant enemies and take them down.
CASEY, STAY AWAY! IT'S GOT A LONG REACH!
YOU STRENGTHENED GROOKEY'S STICK, BUT BE CAREFUL—DREDNAW MIGHT CHOMP IT!
GROOKEY, LET GO OF YOUR STICK!
YOU'LL NEVER YANK IT FREE OF DRED-NAW'S JAWS!
IT'LL BE OKAY! I CAN FIX IT AFTER THE BATTLE!

BUOOSH
SHF
SHF SHF
THE BURNED DREDNAW IS SLOWING DOWN! KEEP IT BUSY WHILE IT WEARS ITSELF OUT!
GST
OH NO, SCOR-BUNNY!
KRRRN
IT BIT ITS FLAME POUCH!
CHH

WHAT'S A FLAME POUCH?
AN ORGAN FOR FIRE, LIKE A SECOND HEART.
OH NO...
SOBBLE, WHERE'D YOU COME FROM?
GRRRR...
LOOK OUT!
CLOMP
CLOMP
CLOMP
CLOMP
FWOO
FWOO
FWOOM
FWOOM

SPLOOSH
SOBBLE DISAP-PEARED ?!
ZHEEN
UMP
STAGGER
STAGGER

GROOKEY, NOW!
WHERE DID SOBBLE GO?!
SOBBLE BECOMES INVISIBLE WHEN IT GETS WET.
UM...
IT'S RIGHT HERE.
FWOO
FWOO
FWOOOM

IF YOU AND SOBBLE AGREE, THERE'S NOTHING TO STOP YOU!
ME ?!
RE-ALLY ?!
MARVIN, WOULD YOU LIKE TO TAKE CARE OF SOBBLE?
...
WHAT DO YOU THINK, SOBBLE?
BMP
BMP

VRROOM
MEANWHILE, AT TURF-FIELD...
MILO! MILO!
TURF-FIELD STADIUM
DID YOU HEAR?!
LEON!
YEAH, I HEARD.
LEON RECOM-MENDED TWO TRAINERS FOR THE GYM CHALLENGE, RIGHT?
IT'S NOT LIKE HIM TO DO THAT.
TURFFIELD STADIUM GYM LEADER: MILO

THE CHAMPION RECOMMENDED A CHALLENGER? TWO OF THEM?
HULBURY STADIUM GYM LEADER: NESSA
REGARDLESS OF WHOEVER RECOMMENDED THEM, I WILL FIGHT THEM WITH EVERYTHING I'VE GOT LIKE I ALWAYS DO.
MOTOSTOKE STADIUM GYM LEADER: KABU
HOW INTER-ESTING.
BALLONLEA STADIUM GYM LEADER: OPAL
THE NEWS OF THE UN-DEFEATED CHAMPION, LEON, RECOM-MENDING NEW CHALLENG-ERS...
...QUICKLY TRAVELED THROUGH THE STADIUMS OF GALAR.

THE SECRETS OF DYNAMAX, PART 3

Wild Area

The Wild Area is known to have many Power Spots. Inhabited by countless Pokémon, anyone who comes near a Power Spot risks a Dynamax battle.

▲ A pillar of red light emanates from a Power Spot in the Wild Area.

THE SOB.
HIS SOBBLE-NESS.
EL SOBBER-INO...
NO, THAT'S TOO LONG.
MORN-ING!
WHAT ARE YOU TWO DOING?
GOOD MORNING, CASEY.
HENRY AND I WERE COMING UP WITH NICKNAMES FOR SOBBLE.
ONCE WE START HAVING GYM BATTLES, WE'LL MEET MANY OTHER TRAINERS.
GROOKEY, SCRATCH!
GROOKEY, BRANCH POKE!
?!
IT MIGHT BE CONFUSING WHEN WE END UP FACING A TRAINER WITH THE SAME KIND OF POKÉMON.
Happens all the time, right?
AND HAVE YOU DECIDED ON NAMES?

A Rising Beam of Light

Adventure 4 Zap!!

OH WOW!
IT'S A PRISTINE WILDERNESS FULL OF WILD POKÉMON.
WHAT'S THE WILD AREA...?
YOU ARE FREE TO TRAIN AND CAPTURE NEW POKÉMON HERE.
BUT YOU COULD RUN INTO SOME EXTREMELY STRONG POKÉMON...
...SO YOU NEED TO BE CARE-FUL.
CASEY, LET'S START OUR INVESTIGA-TION FROM THE ROLLING FIELDS.
YOU BET!
SO HER RESEARCH INTO DYNAMAX BRINGS HER HERE...
...TO THE WILD AREA?
INVESTI-GATION?
OF COURSE! WE'RE HERE BECAUSE OF PRO-FESSOR MAGNOLIA'S RESEARCH!

DYNAMAXING IS CONNECTED TO THE POWER SPOTS...
...AND THE WILD AREA IS FULL OF POWER SPOTS!
YOU CAN EITHER WANDER AROUND LOOKING FOR THEM...
...OR YOU CAN USE THE POWER SPOT DETECTOR!
TA-DA!
THE ROLLING FIELDS HAVE NINE POWER SPOTS IN TOTAL!
WHAT'S A POKÉMON DEN?
THAT'S WHAT WE CALL THE POWER SPOTS IN THE WILD AREA.
DO YOU SEE THAT PILLAR OF LIGHT?
YES!
LET'S INVESTIGATE EACH POKÉMON DEN AND FIND OUT WHAT KIND OF POKÉMON LIVES THERE.

A POKÉMON LITERALLY LIVES INSIDE IT.
BELOW THAT LIGHT...
...WILL BE A DYNA-MAXED POKÉ-MON.
THAT'S A REAL DYNAMAXED POKÉMON!
GULP
NOT A VR ONE LIKE I SAW YESTER-DAY!
ENTERING A DEN MEANS WE'LL HAVE TO FIGHT THAT POKÉMON!
AND IF WE WIN, WE CAN CAPTURE IT!
THAT'S A BIG IF!
AS FOR TODAY, WE CAME HERE TO GATHER DATA.
PLEASE DON'T IMME-DIATELY CHARGE INTO THE DENS.
IS THERE ANY WAY TO KNOW WHAT SORT OF POKÉMON IS IN THE DEN?
THE APP IN OUR ROTOM PHONE WILL TELL US IF WE GET CLOSE ENOUGH!
DING! ♪

MAIL!
OVER HERE!
FLAP
FLAP
FLAP
THANKS!
TMP!
I LOVE GETTING MAIL!
CASEY SH
THANK YOU!

HEY, IT'S FROM THE GYM CHALLENGE OFFICE!
TA-DA!
UNI-FORMS?
OFFICIAL UNI-FORMS! OUR CHAL-LENGE BANDS WERE INSIDE TOO!
IS THERE A MEANING BEHIND THE UNIFORM NUMBER?
I LOVE PALIN-DROMES. ♡
303
OFFICIAL PARTICI-PANTS WEAR THE UNIFORM FOR GYM BATTLES.
I GUESS THAT MEANS WE'RE OFFICIAL!
808

LET'S TRY THEM ON AND SEE IF THEY FIT!
GOOD IDEA!
USH!
WHOA! WHOA!
ISH!!
HEY!
BE CAREFUL! YOU MIGHT RIP IT!
RIP IT?!
YOU'LL RIP YOUR LIP IF YOU KEEP YAPPIN'!
JUST GIVE UP NOW!
YOU'LL NEVER WIN YOUR GYM CHAL-LENGE, HENRY SWORD AND CASEY SHIELD!
WHAT ARE YOU TALKING ABOUT?!

HOW DO YOU KNOW WHO WE ARE?
TWO YOUNG TRAINERS RECOMMENDED BY THE CHAMP HIMSELF...
...SAID TO BE TRAVELIN' WITH PROFESSOR MAGNOLIA IN AN RV!
IT'S THE BIGGEST NEWS IN GALAR!
THAT'S WHY WE'RE HERE TO STOP YOU!
WE'RE TEAM YELL!
YOU'RE TRYING TO STOP US FROM CARRYING OUT OUR GYM CHALLENGE?!
THAT'S RIGHT!
DO IT, LINOONE!
GO, THIEVUL!

SUCKER PUNCH!
LANCE-LOT!
NIGHT SLASH!
WHAT IS YOUR PROBLEM?!
TEAM YELL MAKES SURE OUR PRINCESS WINS!
WHAT PRIN-CESS?!

BOW BEFORE OUR PRINCESS! THE ONE AND ONLY...
... MARNIE !!
YOU EXPECT ME TO BELIEVE A PRINCESS TOLD YOU TO COME BULLY US?!
GASP!
SUCH DISRE-SPECT!
MARNIE WOULD NEVER TELL US TO DO SOMETHING SO WRONG!
SO YOU KNOW THIS IS WRONG!

WE MUST ENSURE MARNIE'S VICTORY!
WE FORBID YOUR SUCCESS!
THIS CONVER-SATION IS ABSURD!
SCOR-BUNNY!
LINOONE HAS BEEN BURNED!
ONCE MORE!
SHFF

SHA
THUNGK
THAT LINOONE HAS QUICK FEET, A HIDDEN ABILITY!
ITS SPEED INCREASED BECAUSE IT HAS A STATUS CONDITION!
NO WAY!
...
TWIGGY ...
PSST, PSST.

THK
THK
OW!
AIYEE!
YOU'RE NOT ALLOWED TO ATTACK THE TRAINER!
CASEY, TAKE THIS.
OKAY!
KLIK!
KLIKT!
HEY!
THK
CUT IT OUT!
CSH
WOO!

SHWOOM!
THEY DISAP-PEARED!
HENRY, CASEY, TEAM YELL AND THEIR POKÉMON TOO!
WHAT'S GOING ON?
WHAT WILL THEY HAVE TO BATTLE?!
RR
MM...
RRM BB...
RRM BB BL L

RRMMBBBL
SO THIS IS A DEN, HUH?
IT'S HUGE!
AHHH!
HOW DARE YOU DRAG US DOWN HERE!
WE CAN'T GET OUT UNLESS WE FIGHT THAT DYNAMAXED GURDURR!
THAT'S RIGHT.

WE'LL HAVE TO FIGHT TO-GETHER.
GRRR ...!
WHUMP
AIYEEEE!
IT FLAT-TENED LINOONE WITH ONE HIT!
MY TURN!
THIEVUL, FIRE FANG!

KRRSH!
CHOMP!
GLOMP!
SCOR-BUNNY, EMBER!
SURE THING!
CHOOM
CHOOM
CHOOM
CHOOM
CHOOM
THAT ONLY MADE THINGS WORSE. I GUESS ITS ABILITY IS GUTS.
HOW ARE YOU SO CALM ?!
USE FIRE FANG AGAIN!
BUT THIS TIME, ATTACK ITS GEAR, THE STEEL BEAM.
YOU TOO, SHIELD.

SHWAAA
SHFF
THUNGKT!!
KEEP HEATING THE STEEL BEAM WITH SCORBUNNY'S FIRE!
KEEP ATTACKING, CASEY!
THIEVUL HAS BEEN DEFEAT-ED!

GRRRGH!
FWOOSH
SIZZLE
SIZZLE
THE STEEL BEAM'S HEATIN' UP!
EXACTLY.
NOW, LANCELOT!
USE BRAVE BIRD!
SWIP!

KRR-THUNK!!
FWUMP!
KCH...
GOOD!
KRTCH
KRTCH

TMP
LET'S DO IT!
SHOOOOM
KLIKT
THU NGK

GURDURR.
NOW POCKET-SIZE!
THANK YOU VERY MUCH FOR YOUR HELP.
OH, GROSS!
YOU SURE HANDLED THOSE GOONS, AND...
I MANAGED TO CAPTURE A GURDURR! I'VE ALWAYS WANTED ONE!
WAY TO GO, HENRY!
WHAT'LL YOU CALL IT?
I THINK I'LL CALL HIM STEELER.

YOU KNEW THERE WAS A GURDURR INSIDE THE DEN?
MY APP TOLD ME.
HMPH...
I THOUGHT I TOLD YOU NOT TO JUMP INSIDE THE DEN...
BUT SINCE YOU MANAGED TO CAPTURE GURDURR, THAT MEANS THE DYNAMAX BAND WORKED.
YEP!
LIKE A DREAM!
UM... WHAT IS THE DYNAMAX BAND?
SINCE YOU'RE A MEMBER OF OUR TEAM NOW...
...I THINK IT'S TIME I TOLD YOU ABOUT EVERYTHING.

THE SECRETS OF DYNAMAX, PART 4

▲ Pluck up the courage to jump inside and battle a giant!

Den

A pillar of red light means you've found a Pokémon Den! A powerful Dynamaxed Pokémon will be waiting for you inside!

Hidenori Kusaka is the writer for *Pokémon Adventures*. Running continuously for over 20 years, *Pokémon Adventures* is the only manga series to completely cover all the *Pokémon* games and has become one of the most popular series of all time. In addition to writing manga, he also edits children's books and plans mixed-media projects for Shogakukan's children's magazines. He uses the Pokémon Electrode as his author portrait.

Satoshi Yamamoto is the artist for *Pokémon Adventures*, which he began working on in 2001, starting with volume 10. Yamamoto launched his manga career in 1993 with the horror-action title *Kimen Senshi*, which ran in Shogakukan's *Weekly Shonen Sunday* magazine, followed by the series *Kaze no Denshosha*. Yamamoto's favorite manga creators/artists include Fujiko Fujio (*Doraemon*), Yukinobu Hoshino (*2001 Nights*) and Katsuhiro Otomo (*Akira*). He loves films, monsters, detective novels and punk rock music. He uses the Pokémon Swalot as his artist portrait.

Pokémon: Sword & Shield
Volume 1
VIZ Media Edition

Story by HIDENORI KUSAKA
Art by SATOSHI YAMAMOTO

Original Cover Design—Hiroyuki KAWASOME (grafio)

Translation—Tetsuichiro Miyaki
English Adaptation—Molly Tanzer
Touch-Up & Lettering—Annaliese "Ace" Christman
Design—Alice Lewis
Editor—Joel Enos

Printed in the U.S.A.

Published by VIZ Media, LLC
P.O. Box 77010
San Francisco, CA 94107

10 9 8 7 6 5 4 3 2 1
First printing, August 2021

PARENTAL ADVISORY
POKÉMON: SWORD & SHIELD is rated A and is suitable for readers of all ages.

viz.com

Coming Next Volume

Volume 2

Henry, Casey and their friends arrive at Motostoke to participate in the Gym Challenge. They've missed the opening ceremonies, but they're still able to join in the challenges! Henry's first official battle pits him against Gym Leader Milo.

Will Henry's first Dynamax battle also be his last?!

READ THIS WAY!

THIS IS THE END OF THIS GRAPHIC NOVEL!

To properly enjoy this VIZ Media graphic novel, please turn it around and begin reading from right to left.

This book has been printed in the original Japanese format in order to preserve the orientation of the original artwork. H[illegible]

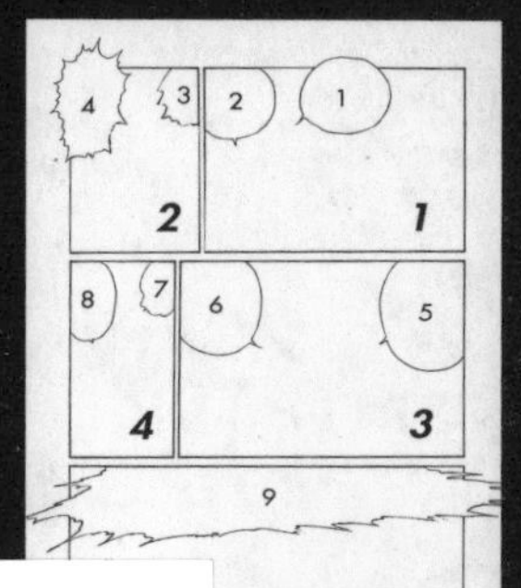

[illegible]e action this way.